cloverleaf books™

Where I Live

This Is My Continent

Lisa Bullard

illustrated by **Paula Becker**

M MILLBROOK PRESS · MINNEAPOLIS

Chapter One
Astronaut Adventure

My babysitter, Ruby, and I are playing our favorite game. We're astronauts! Ruby salutes me. "Captain Noah! We have time for one last adventure before bedtime. What's it going to be?"

"Let's explore the entire planet!" I say.

"Aye, aye, sir," says Ruby. "I think we have just enough time to check out all the continents!"

A continent is a very large area of land. There are seven continents on Earth.

Chapter Two

Asia to Antarctica

I steer our spaceship close to the biggest continent. Ruby's job is to be our fact finder. She pulls out her SpacePhone to look up facts about continents. "This continent is called Asia," she says. "More than half the people in the world live here."

We fly on to Europe, Asia's neighbor. Ruby says the two continents even share some countries. "Europeans have really gotten around," she says. "At different times, they have ruled all or part of most other continents."

Mountains separate much of Europe from Asia. Other continents, like Africa and South America, are separated by the sea.

8

We circle around the top of the Eiffel Tower in France.

Then we speed along the fjords of Norway.

Next, we zoom south to Africa. We fly across the Sahara, a giant desert. I buzz over the tops of the pyramids.

"Africa has more than fifty countries," reads Ruby. "That's more than any other continent. And about two thousand languages are spoken here!"

Cape Town, South Africa

Earth did not always have seven continents. Long ago, today's continents were just one giant continent. Smaller continents broke off from it and drifted apart.

We speed across an ocean to another continent. "This is Australia," Ruby says. "And this dry land in the center is called the outback."

"I see lots more kangaroos here than people," I say.

Ruby tells me most Australians live in cities near the ocean. We find plenty of people near the Sydney Opera House.

We fly even farther south. "This is the continent of Antarctica," says Ruby. "Ice covers most of it all year. And temperatures can fall below -90° Celsius. That's -130° Fahrenheit!"

Antarctica has no countries or cities. The only people there are scientists. *Brrrr!* We shiver and wave good-bye to the penguins.

Chapter Three

The Americas

We head to South America. I fly straight to the Amazon rain forest. We can warm up there! Ruby says, "This rain forest has more kinds of plants and animals than anywhere else on Earth."

Bogotá

Amazon River

Amazon Rain Forest

The Andes

Buenos Aires

Rio de Janeiro

We zoom over the ancient city of Machu Picchu.

In a newer city named Bogotá, Colombia, some kids call out "Hola!" Ruby says Spanish and Portuguese are South America's most common languages.

Indigenous peoples built Machu Picchu and other ancient cities in South America. Indigenous peoples have lived on most continents for thousands of years.

Now it's time to check out our own continent! We fly up a land bridge to North America. "The United States is a powerful country," Ruby says. "But there are many other interesting places in North America. It also includes Central America, the Caribbean, Mexico, Canada, and Greenland."

Greenland

The Great Lakes

The Rocky Mountains

New York City

The Grand Canyon

The Mississippi River

The Alamo

Mexico

Continents also include nearby islands. Greenland is the world's largest island.

We fly over Mexico City, the biggest city in North America. We zoom along the Golden Gate Bridge. We buzz over the Canadian Rockies.

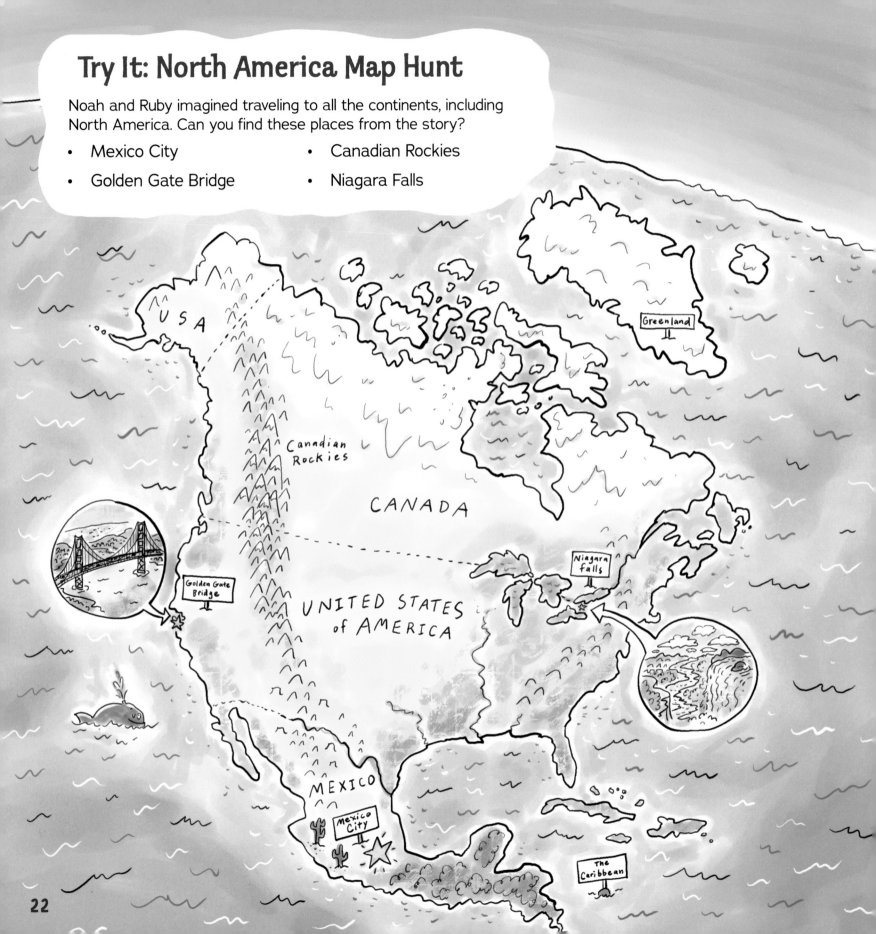

Try It: North America Map Hunt

Noah and Ruby imagined traveling to all the continents, including North America. Can you find these places from the story?

- Mexico City
- Golden Gate Bridge
- Canadian Rockies
- Niagara Falls

GLOSSARY

ancient: very old

city: an area with many buildings and people. Cities have names and governments.

continent: a large landmass. Earth's continents are Africa, Antarctica, Asia, Australia, Europe, North America, and South America.

country: a large section of land with its own government

fjord: a narrow part of the ocean between steep slopes

hola: a word that means "hello" in Spanish

indigenous peoples: groups of people who lived somewhere for a very long time before other people came to live there, such as the Navajo people of the United States

outback: the dry inland area of Australia

pyramid: a human-made structure with sloping sides that meet in a point at the top

rain forest: a very wet forest with lots of plants and animals

BOOKS

Boothroyd, Jennifer. *Map My Continent*. Minneapolis: Lerner Publications, 2014. Learn more about continents in this fun book.

Kalman, Bobbie. *Explore Earth's Seven Continents*. New York: Crabtree, 2011. The photos, maps, and interesting facts in this book will teach you more about the continents.

National Geographic Society. *National Geographic Kids Beginner's World Atlas*. Washington, DC: National Geographic Society, 2011. Learn more about the continents through the information, photographs, and maps in this book.

WEBSITES

Enchanted Learning: The Continents
http://www.enchantedlearning.com/geography/continents
Visit Enchanted Learning for quizzes, activities, and fact sheets related to the continents.

Kids Do Ecology: World Biomes
http://kids.nceas.ucsb.edu/biomes
This website will help you learn about the parts of the different continents that have similar climates, plants, and animals.

***Time for Kids*—Around the World**
http://www.timeforkids.com/around-the-world
This site offers a collection of facts and photos from places around the world.

LERNER SOURCE™
Expand learning beyond the printed book. Download free, complementary educational resources for this book from our website, www.lerneresource.com.